Goodnight Surf City

Toni Haas
Goodnight Surf City

PALMETTO
PUBLISHING
Charleston, SC
www.PalmettoPublishing.com

Hardcover ISBN: 979-8-8229-2542-7
Paperback ISBN: 979-8-8229-2543-4

Dedicated to my wonderful grandchildren from near and far. You will always have fun memories when visiting me and some of our favorite spots in Huntington Beach, California.

Love you,
Grandma, a.k.a. Grandma T~

Goodnight Pacific
Coast Highway,

at the end of a perfect day.

Goodnight beaches,

the dolphins were the best.
Now it's time to go home and rest.

Goodnight kites,
you've all flown away.

We'll come back again another day.

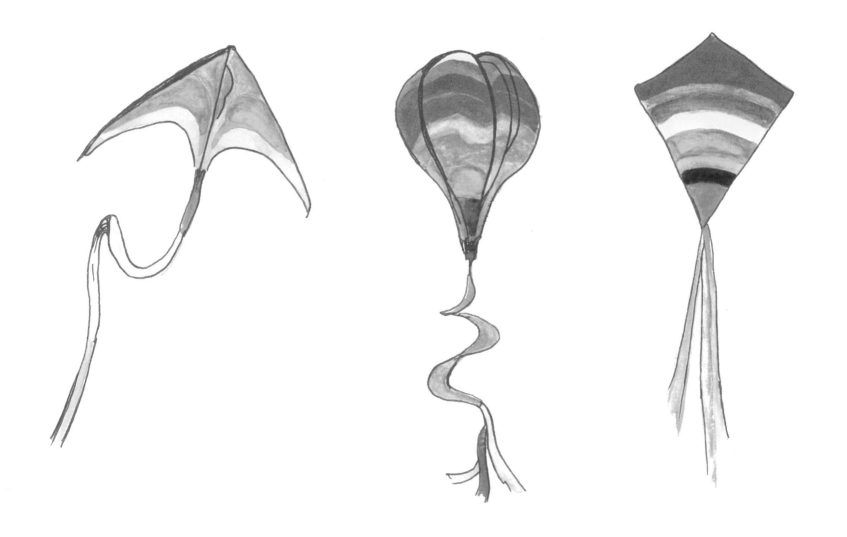

Goodnight, Surf Museum.

Your stories of the past
and preserving history,
will always last.

It's the perfect spot to go explore!

Goodnight summer nights

and bonfire lights.

where the pups love to play
and romp in the waves all day.

Time to recover from all the fun.

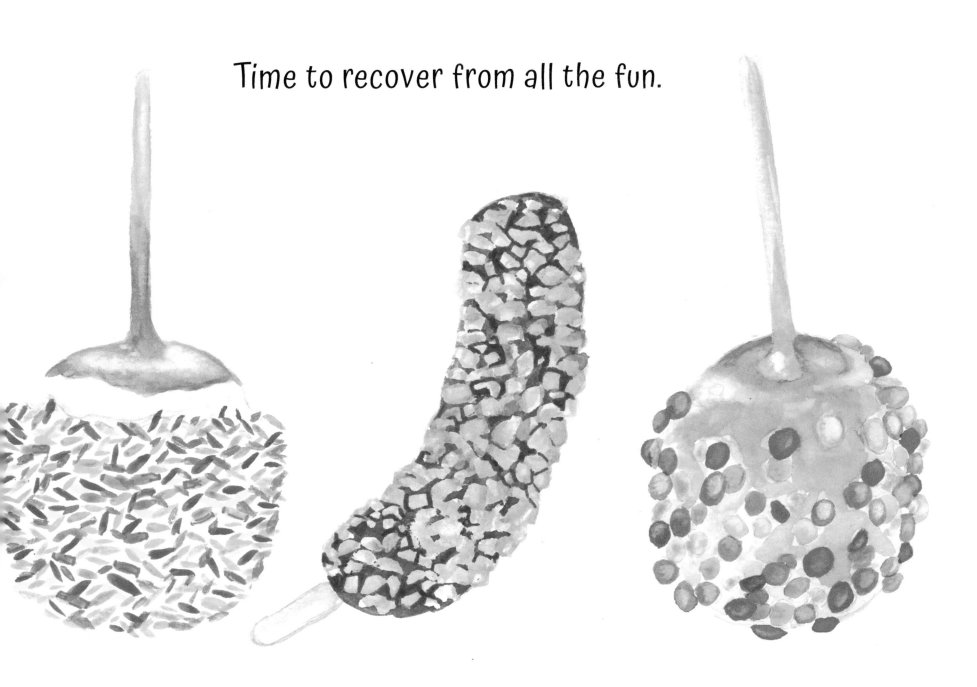

Goodnight skate park.
We'll see you soon.

Goodnight tacos,
my favorite food.

So tasty and always good.

Goodnight kayaking,

thank you for the fun ride.
It's time to paddle back in with the tide.

Goodnight Central Park,
where the ducks have gone to rest,

until tomorrow when they'll wake from their nest.

Goodnight wetlands,
a home to birds and more.

You are a super fun place to explore!

Goodnight Huntington Beach Pier,

your view of the Pacific so magical and clear.

Goodnight surf shops, with your boards and wax.

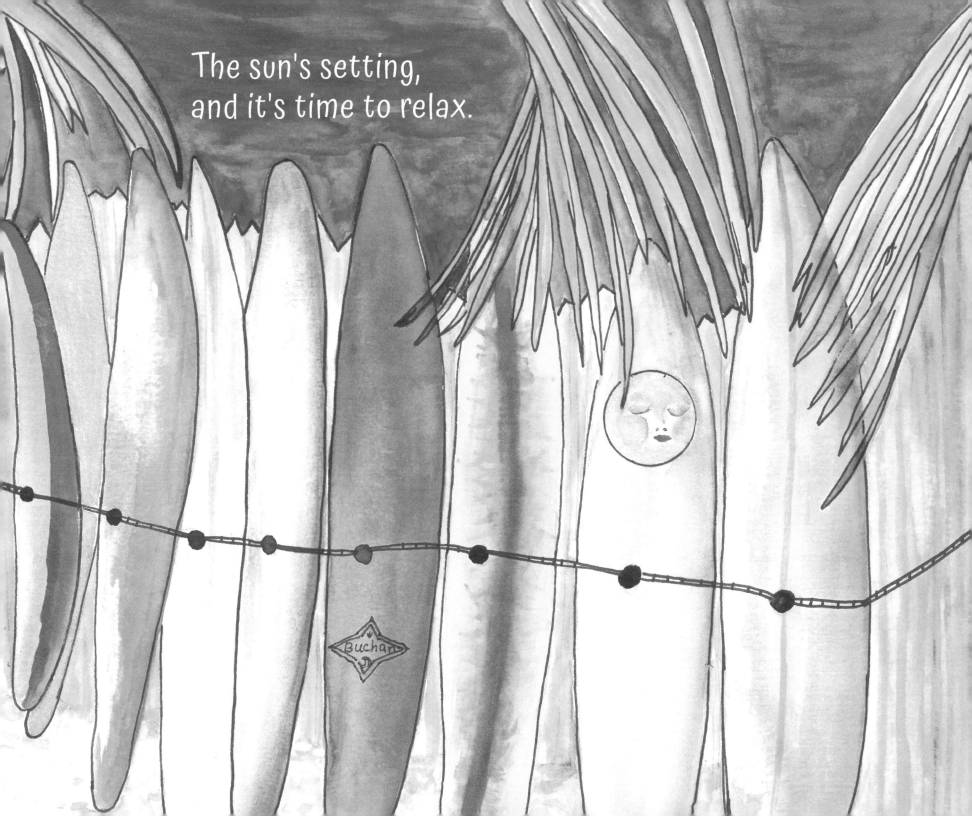

Goodnight and Goodbye PCH.

GOOD
NIGHT

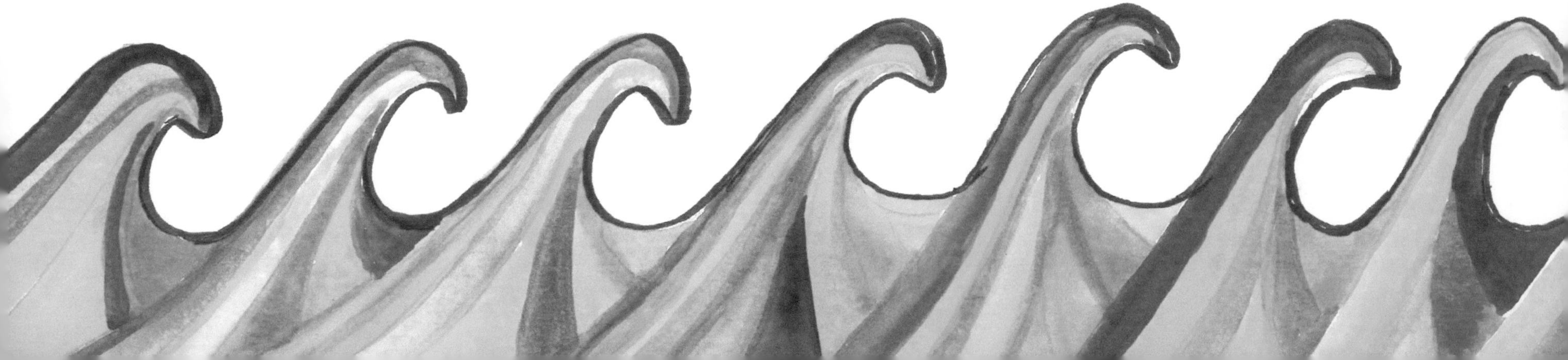

About the Author

Toni Haas, a fifth-generation Southern Californian, beautifully intertwines her love for art and her deep roots in Huntington Beach within her work. Growing up in the San Bernardino Mountains and having spent numerous summers in Huntington Beach before making it her home in the late 80's, Toni's connection with the locale shines brightly in her narratives. Today, Toni cherishes moments with her grandchildren. For Toni, life is about family, nature, and making unforgettable memories.

Printed in the USA
CPSIA information can be obtained
at www.ICGtesting.com
LVHW071935310524
781931LV00004B/81

9 798822 925434